fiddle-i-fee

a noisy nursery rhyme by
Jakki Wood

Bradbury Press New York

I had a cat, the cat pleased me,
I fed my cat by the old oak tree.
Cat went fiddle-i-fee.

I had a hen, the hen pleased me,
I fed my hen by the old oak tree.
Hen went chimmey-chuck
chimmey-chuck...

cat went fiddle-i-fee.

I had a rooster, the rooster pleased me,
I fed my rooster by the old oak tree.
Rooster went doodle-do...

I had a goose, the goose pleased me,
I fed my goose by the old oak tree.

Goose went swishy-swashy splishy-splashy...

I had a goat, the goat pleased me,
I fed my goat by the old oak tree.

Goat went bumpity-bump...

I had a horse, the horse pleased me,
I fed my horse by the old oak tree.
Horse went . . .

trit-trot . . .

I had an owl, the owl pleased me,
my owl sat up in the old oak tree.
Owl went...

tuwit

horse went trit-trot... goat went bumpity-bump...

goose went swishy-swashy splishy-splashy...

and the cat went fiddle-i-fee!

fiddle-i-fee

Fairly quick ♩ = c.160

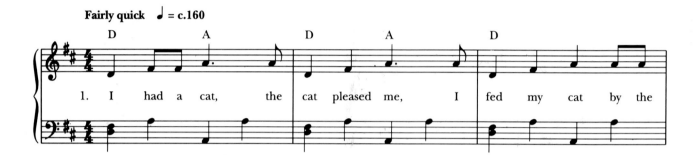

1. I had a cat, the cat pleased me, I fed my cat by the

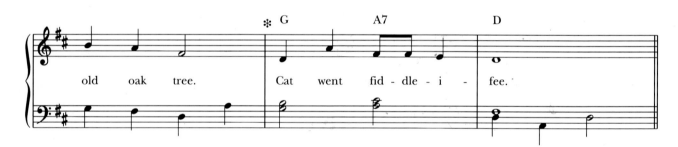

old oak tree. Cat went fid - dle - i - fee.

2. I had a hen, the hen pleased me,
   I fed my hen by the old oak tree.
   Hen went chimmey-chuck chimmey-chuck,
   cat went fiddle-i-fee.

Hen went chim-mey-chuck chim-mey-chuck,

3. I had a rooster, the rooster pleased me,
   I fed my rooster by the old oak tree.
   Rooster went doodle-do,
   hen went chimmey-chuck chimmey-chuck,
   cat went fiddle-i-fee.

Roost - er went doo - dle - do,

* After each new animal verse, repeat all previous noises.

4. I had a goose...

Goose went swi-shy-swa-shy spli-shy-spla-shy,

5. I had a goat...

Goat went bump - i - ty - bump,

6. I had a horse...

Horse went trit - trot,